Dear Parent:
Your child's love of reading starts here!

Every child learns to read in a different way and at his or her own speed. Some go back and forth between reading levels and read favorite books again and again. Others read through each level in order. You can help your young reader improve and become more confident by encouraging his or her own interests and abilities. From books your child reads with you to the first books he or she reads alone, there are I Can Read Books for every stage of reading:

SHARED READING
Basic language, word repetition, and whimsical illustrations, ideal for sharing with your emergent reader

BEGINNING READING
Short sentences, familiar words, and simple concepts for children eager to read on their own

READING WITH HELP
Engaging stories, longer sentences, and language play for developing readers

READING ALONE
Complex plots, challenging vocabulary, and high-interest topics for the independent reader

ADVANCED READING
Short paragraphs, chapters, and exciting themes for the perfect bridge to chapter books

I Can Read Books have introduced children to the joy of reading since 1957. Featuring award-winning authors and illustrators and a fabulous cast of beloved characters, I Can Read Books set the standard for beginning readers.

A lifetime of discovery begins with the magical words "I Can Read!"

Visit www.icanread.com for information on enriching your child's reading experience.

I Can Read Book® is a trademark of HarperCollins Publishers.

Wonder Woman: I Am Wonder Woman
WONDER WOMAN, BATMAN, SUPERMAN, and all related characters and elements are trademarks of DC Comics © 2010. All rights reserved. Printed in the United States of America. No part of this book may be used or reproduced in any manner whatsoever without written permission except in the case of brief quotations embodied in critical articles and reviews. For information address HarperCollins Children's Books, a division of HarperCollins Publishers, 10 East 53rd Street, New York, NY 10022. www.icanread.com

Library of Congress catalog card number: 2010922250
ISBN 978-0-06-188517-4
Typography by John Sazaklis

12   13   14   LP/WOR   10   9   8   7   6   5   ❖   First Edition

I Can Read!™ READING 2 WITH HELP

WONDER WOMAN™

I Am Wonder Woman

Written by Erin K. Stein

Illustrations by Rick Farley

WONDER WOMAN created by William Moulton Marston

HARPER

An Imprint of HarperCollins*Publishers*

My name is Princess Diana.
I grew up in a secret place
called Paradise Island.
I am an Amazon.

My mother is Queen Hippolyta.
She rules the Amazons
and protects Paradise Island.
All Amazons are strong warriors.

The Greek gods told my mother
about the dangers in the world.
Mankind needed someone
to keep the world safe.

The gods wanted to send the best
Amazon warrior to do the job.

The Queen had a contest to see which of us was faster, stronger, and braver than all the others.

Though I was a princess,

I did not want to become queen.

I wanted to fight for justice.

I secretly entered the contest.

I tried my best to win.

All of my arrows hit the target.

I outran all my Amazon sisters.

Our bracelets work as shields.

I moved as fast as lightning

to block all the arrows

fired by my opponents.

In the last sword fight,
I beat all the other finalists.
After I won, I showed my face
to the crowd.

My mother was surprised
but also very proud.
"Diana, you have earned it.
You are a champion," she said.

She gave me a special costume
and a new title to go with it:
Wonder Woman.

The Greek gods gave me

the ability to talk to animals

and a magic lasso

that makes people tell the truth.

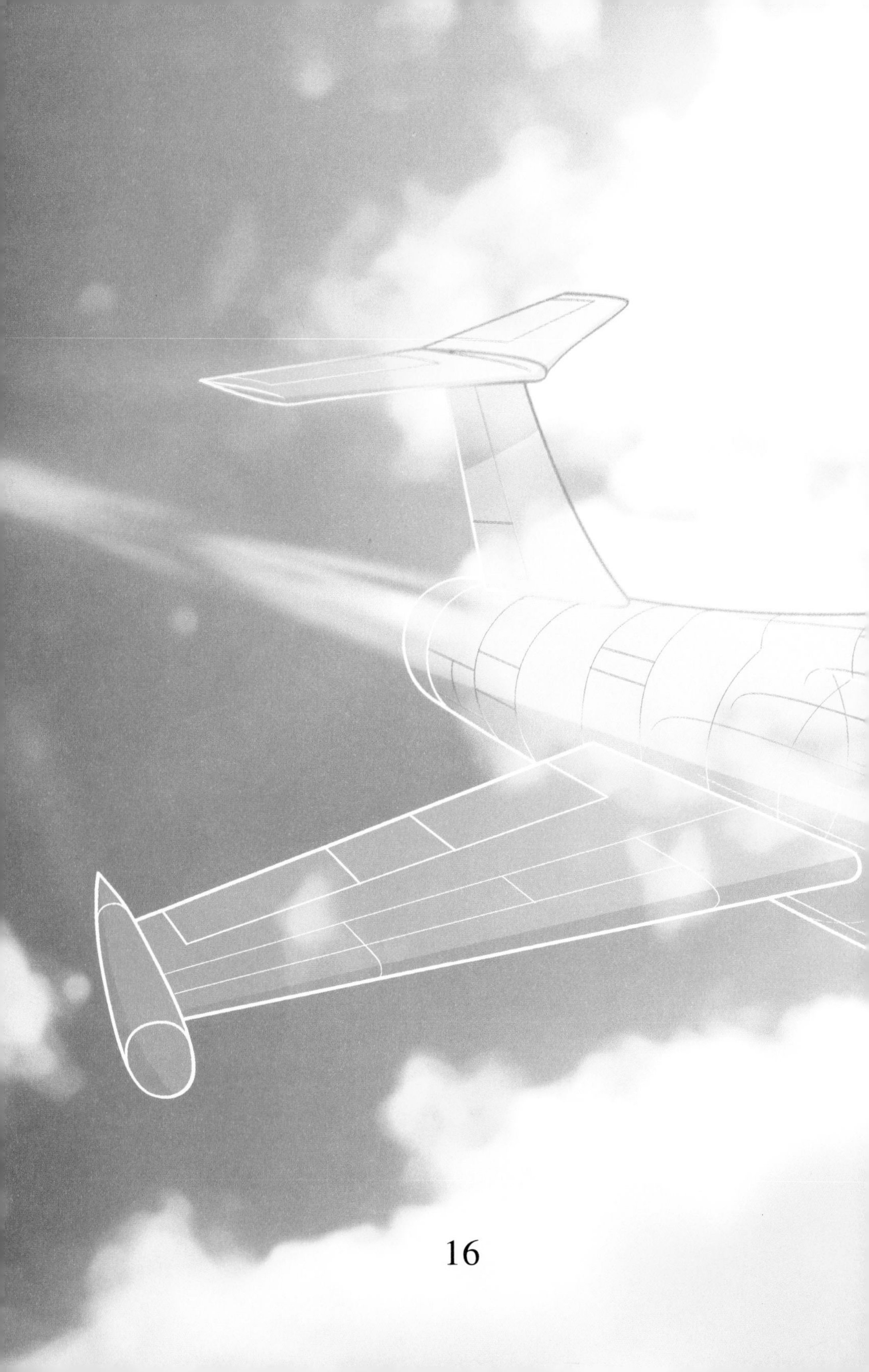

16

To keep Paradise Island a secret,

I fly my Invisible Jet

so no one can see where I go.

I left Paradise Island
to live in Washington, DC.
My secret identity
is Diana Prince.

I work for the government at a top secret agency. At my job, I find out first when there is trouble.

ALERT: ROBBERY IN PROGRESS AT NATIONAL ZOO

CLASSIFIED

Two important reports come in.

An old bridge will collapse

the next time a train goes across.

And there's a crime at the zoo!

I spin very fast to change

into my super hero costume.

I rush to the rescue as Wonder Woman!

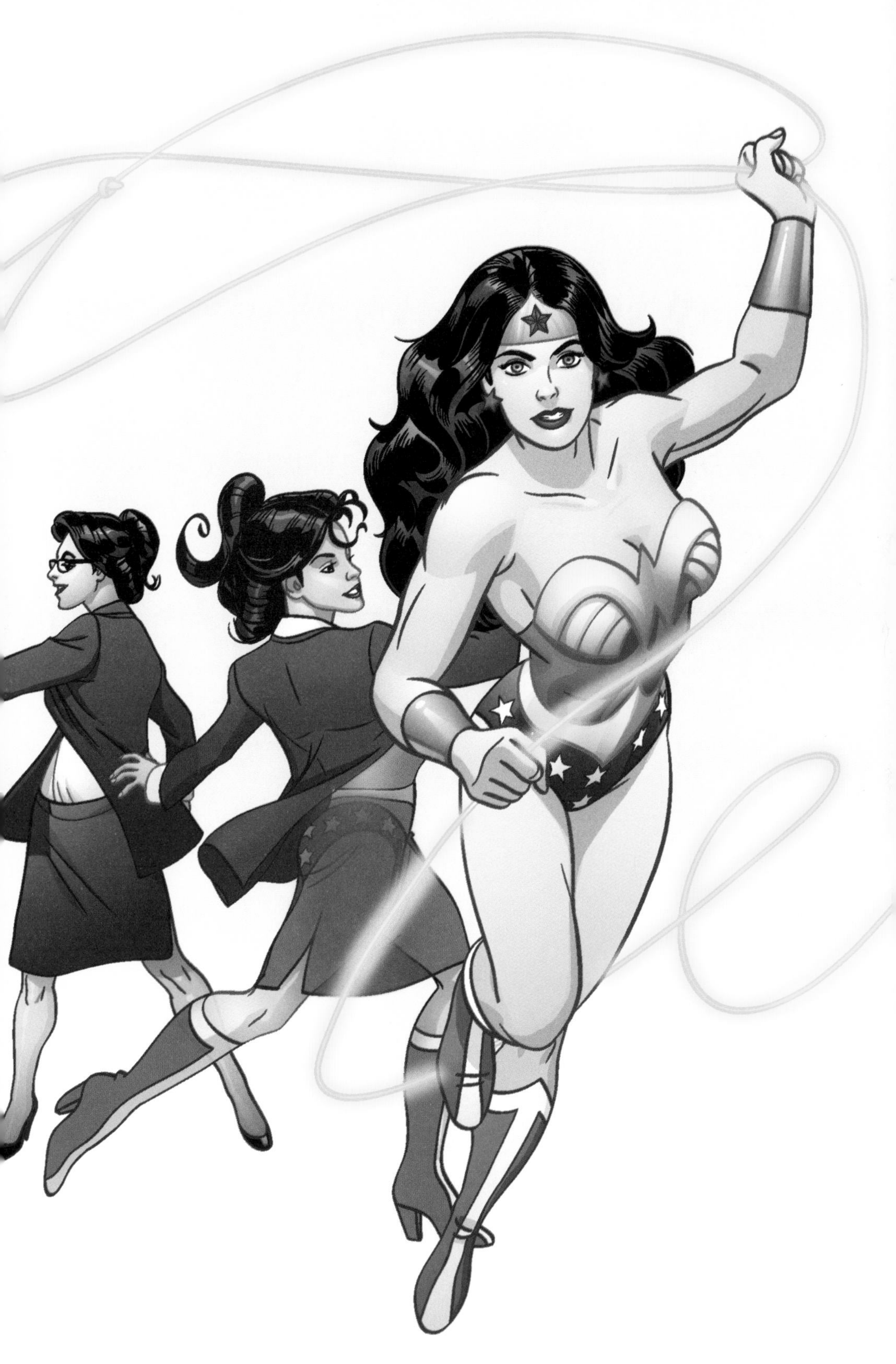

I fly through the city
faster than the speed of sound.
I use my super-strength
to help those in danger.

Just as the bridge collapses
I carry the train to safety.

There's no time to rest.

A tiger was stolen from the zoo!

Two strange men start to run.

"Stop!" I shout.

I toss my Lasso of Truth

and catch the robbers.

The lasso makes them tell me

where they hid the tiger.

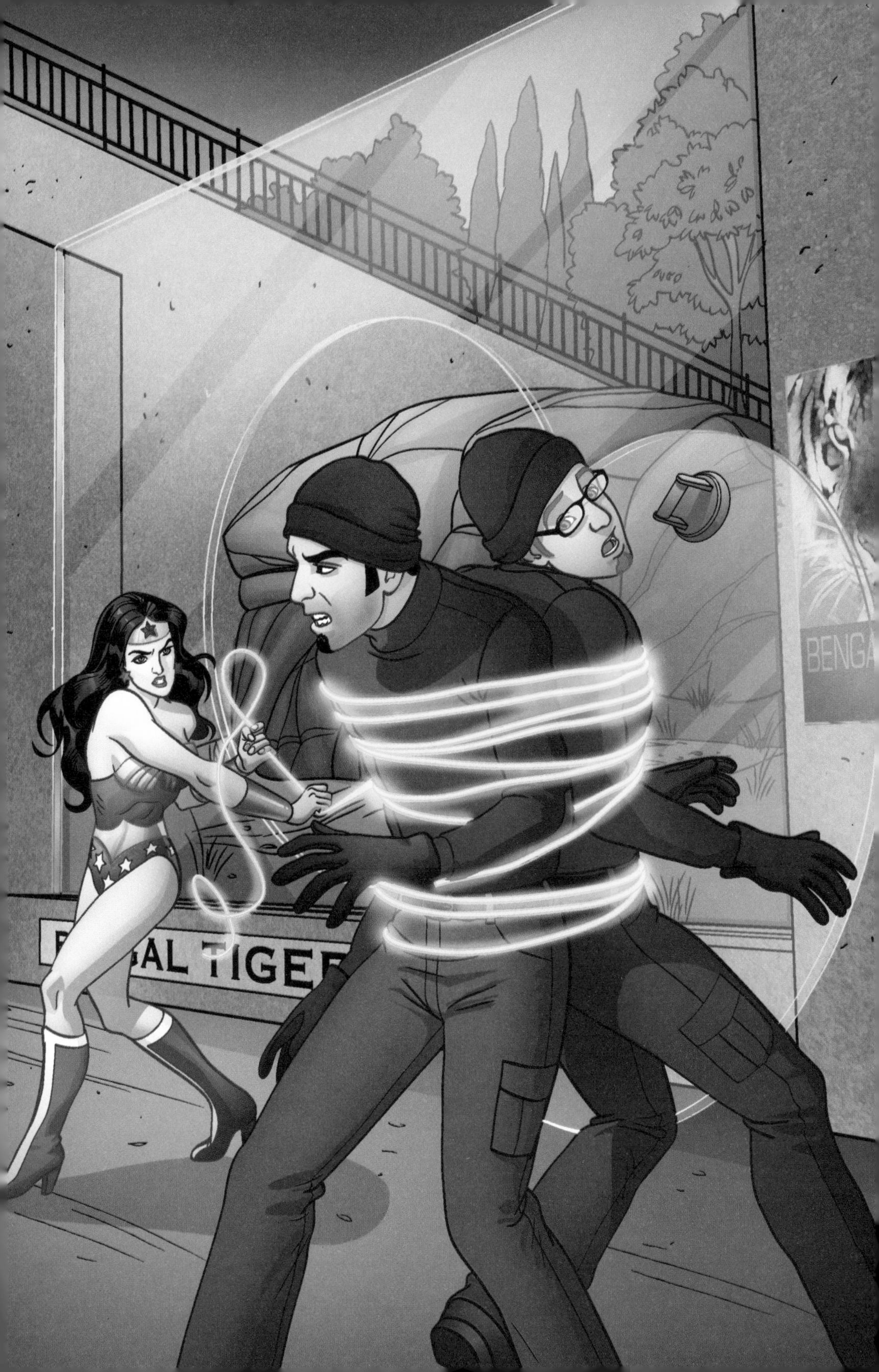

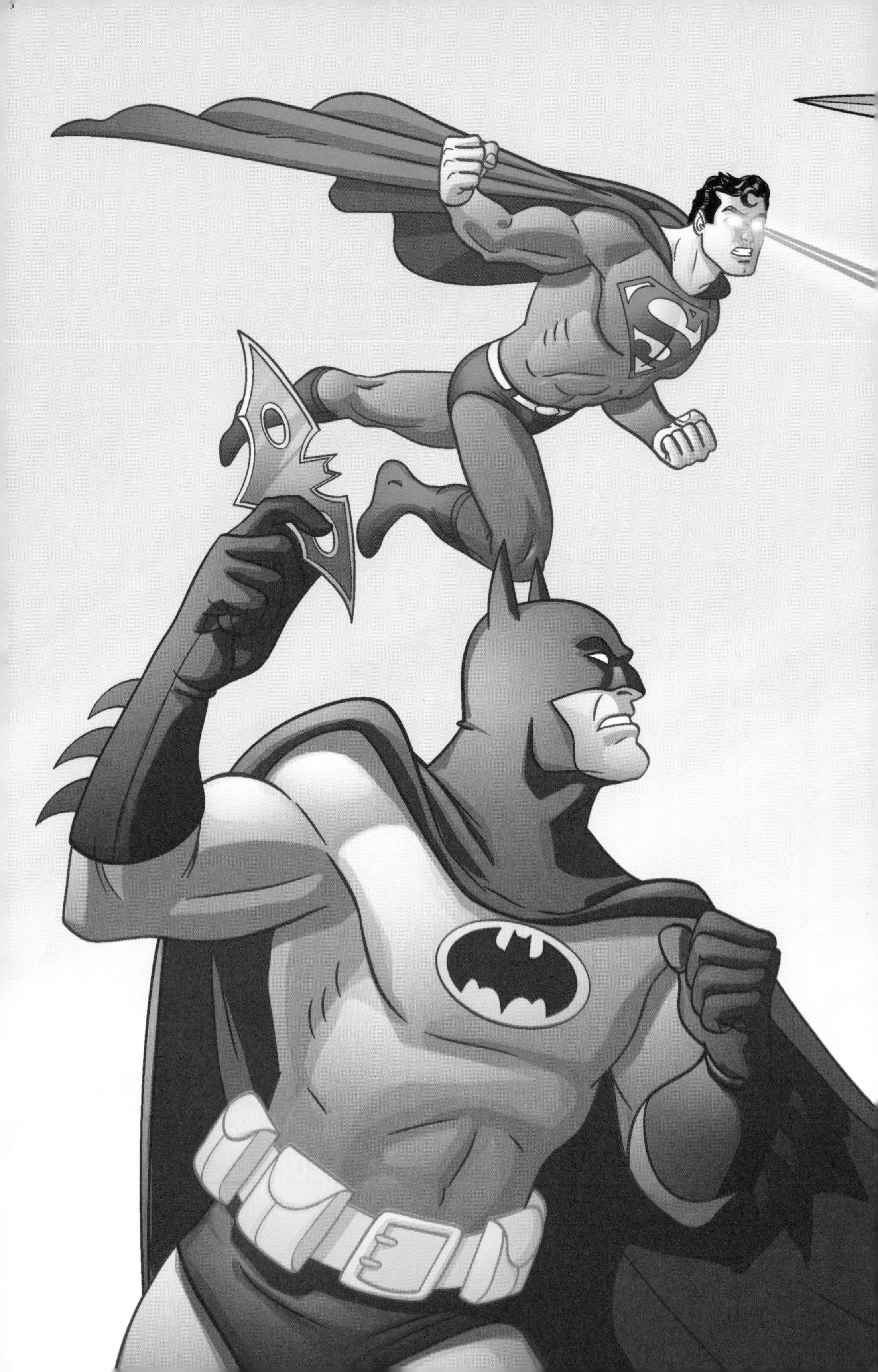

Sometimes I have no choice
but to fight an enemy.

My friends Superman and Batman help
me train for all forms of combat.

Not every crime is easy to stop.

I must be prepared for anything,

even mythical beasts!

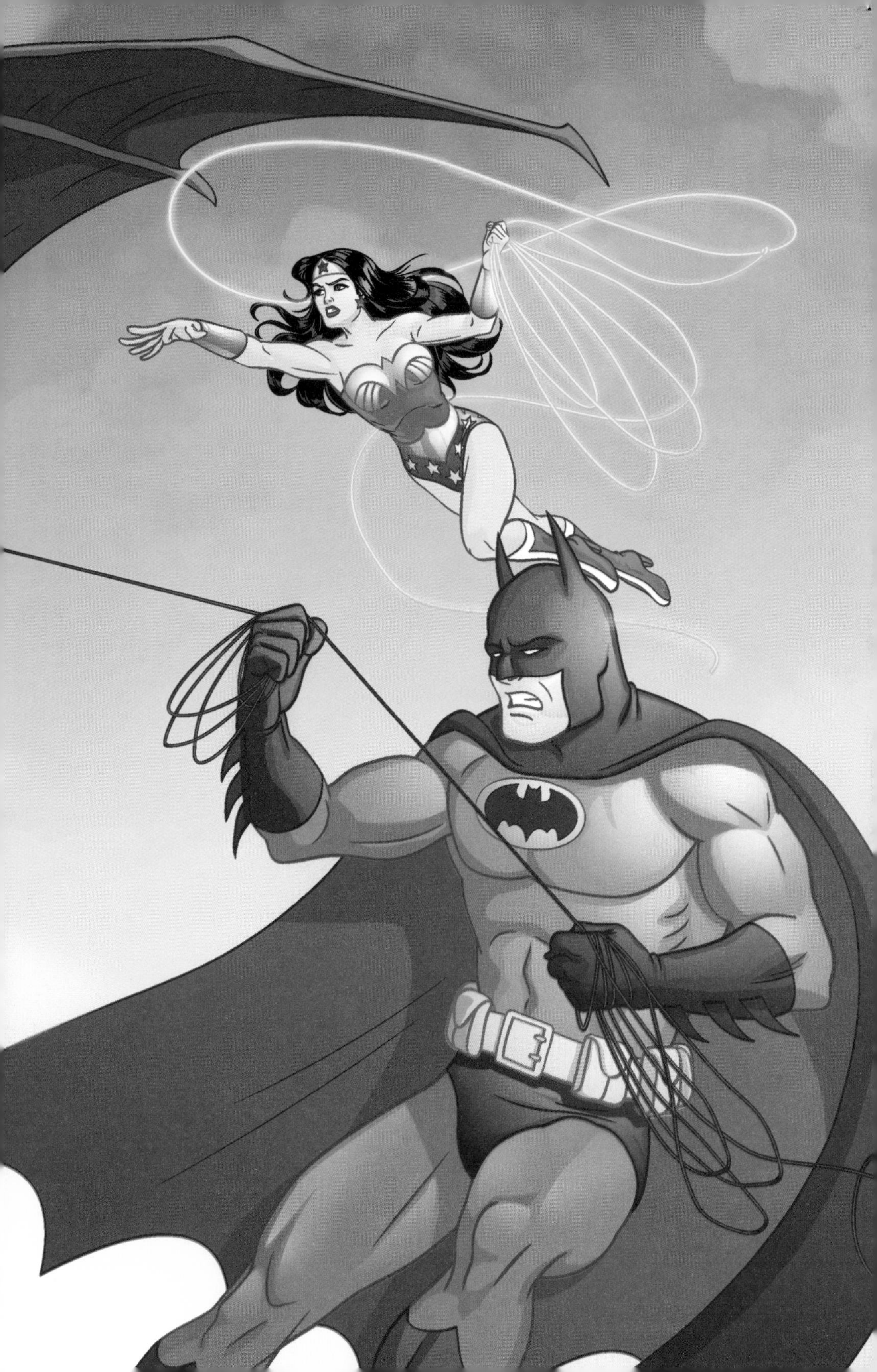

As Wonder Woman, I am famous.

My secret identity

lets me live a normal life, too.

Only my closest friends

know my secret. . . .

I am Wonder Woman!

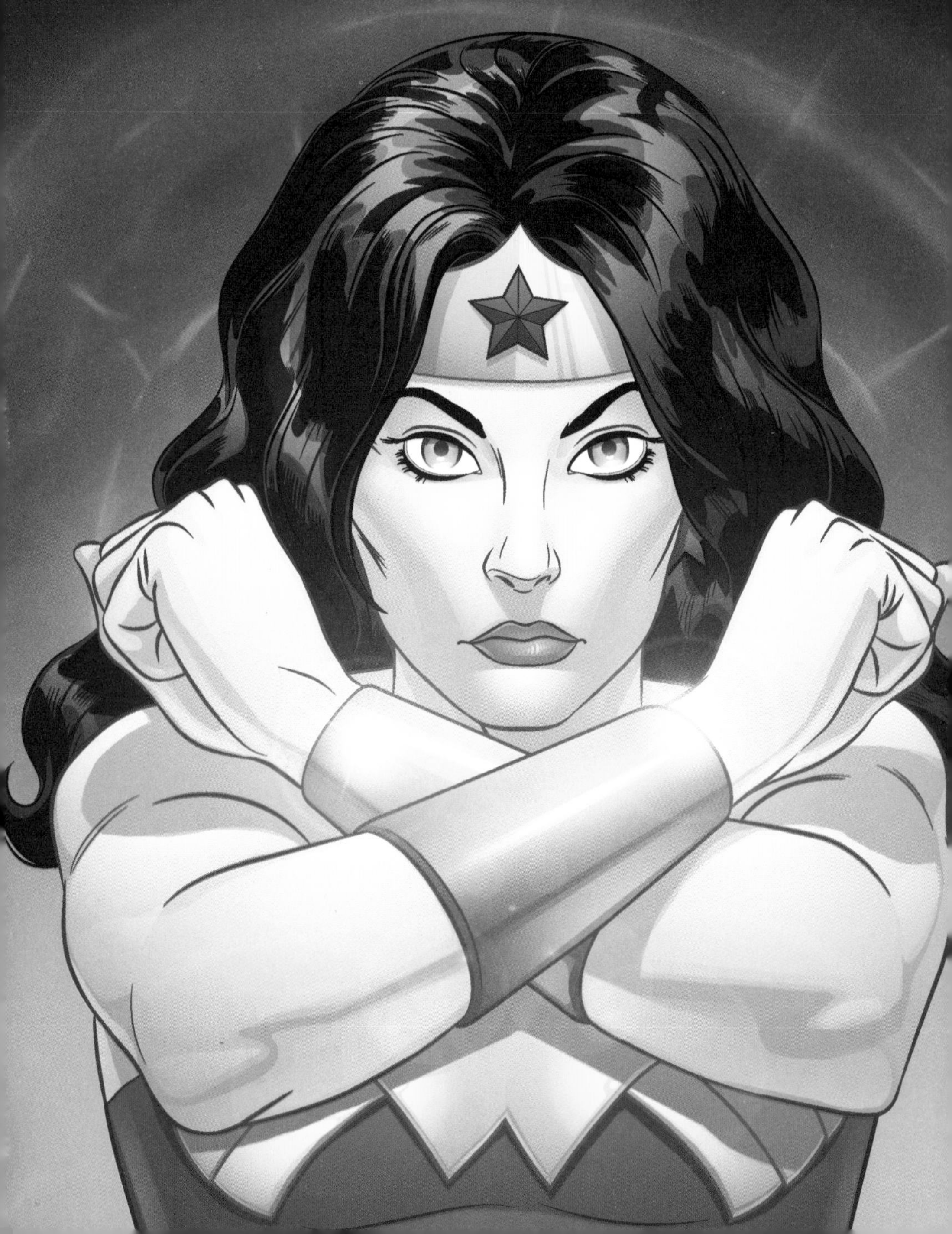